A ROOKIE READER®

KATIE CAN

By Becky Bring McDaniel

Illustrations by Lois Axeman

Prepared under the direction of Robert Hillerich, Ph.D.

CHILDRENS PRESS®

CHICAGO

For Joyce

Library of Congress Cataloging in Publication Data

McDaniel, Becky Bring.
  Katie can.

  (A Rookie Reader)
  Summary: Although she is too small to roller-skate
backwards or ride a bike with no hands, Katie surprises
her older brother and sister when she teaches their dog a
new trick.
  [1. Size—Fiction. 2. Ability—Fiction. 3. Brothers and
sisters—Fiction] I. Axeman, Lois, ill. II. Title.
III. Series.
PZ7.M1399Kat 1987   [E]   87-5190
ISBN 0-516-02082-X

Childrens Press, Chicago
Copyright © 1987 by Regensteiner Publishing Enterprises, Inc.
All rights reserved. Published simultaneously in Canada.
Printed in the United States of America.
    3 4 5 6 7 8 9 10 R 96 95 94 93 92 91 90 89

Jenny was the oldest and the biggest.

Kris was the second oldest and the second biggest.

Katie was the youngest and the smallest.

Jenny could ride her bike with no hands.

Kris could ride his bike with no hands.

Katie said, "I can ride my bike
with no hands."

But when everyone came to
see her, she fell off!

Kris could roller-skate backward.

Jenny could roller-skate backward.

Katie said, "I can roller-skate
backward."

11

But when everyone came to
see her, she fell down!

Jenny could swim from one side of
the pool to the other without stopping.

Kris could swim from one side of the
pool to the other without stopping.

16

Katie said, "I can swim from one side of the pool to the other without stopping."

But when everyone came to see her,
she stopped three times!

Kris taught the dog to chase a ball.

Jenny taught the dog
to bring the ball back.

Katie said, "I can teach the dog a trick too."

But this time nobody came to see her.

Katie threw the ball up
and the dog caught it.

Katie said, "I taught the dog a new trick and nobody came to see me. Nobody ever comes to see me when I really can do something."

Katie threw the ball again.
The dog caught it again. Katie
heard some clapping.

When she turned around,
there stood Jenny and Kris.

They did come to see her after all!

WORD LIST

a	did	nobody	swim
after	do	of	taught
again	dog	off	teach
all	down	oldest	the
and	ever	one	there
around	everyone	other	they
back	fell	pool	this
backward	from	really	three
ball	hands	ride	threw
biggest	heard	roller-skate	time
bike	her	said	times
bring	his	second	to
but	I	see	too
came	it	she	trick
can	Jenny	side	turned
caught	Katie	smallest	up
chase	Kris	some	was
clapping	me	something	when
come	my	stood	with
comes	new	stopped	without
could	no	stopping	youngest

About the Author

Becky Bring McDaniel was born September 16, 1953 in Ashland, Ohio. She has lived in Gainesville, Florida since 1970 and traveled to Europe and the Middle East. Her books, *Katie Did It* and *Katie Couldn't*, have been published by Childrens Press in Chicago, Illinois and included in its Rookie Reader Program. Having established herself as a successful writer of children's books and stories, she still pursues her talents as a poet.

Her poetry has been well received thus far and a sampling of the magazines publishing her works include *Writers' Opportunities*, *Creative Years*, the *National Girl Scout Magazine*, *Alura*, and *Whiskey River*. As if these credentials were not enough in their own right, she also has authored an activity puzzle which was published by *High Adventure* magazine.

Currently residing in Gainesville, Florida in order to attend school, she is establishing herself as an artist deemed to be much in demand during the coming years.

About the Artist

Lois Axeman was born and raised in Chicago, Illinois. She studied art in Chicago at the American Academy, Illinois Institute of Technology, and at the Art Institute. She taught illustration at the University of Illinois Circle Campus for four years. The mother of two grown children and grandmother of one, Lois and her husband, Harvey Retzloff, live in a lakefront building where they both pursue their careers in the graphic arts. They share their home with their Shih Tzu dog Marty and their female cat Charlie. Lois uses her children, her grandchild, and her pets as models for her picture book characters. In their spare time Lois and Harvey enjoy painting, playing tennis, and growing orchids.